ALL
YEAR LONG

ALL YEAR LONG

with illustrations by
Richard Scarry

gb Golden Press • New York
Western Publishing Company, Inc.
Racine, Wisconsin

In the Morning

In the morning, we wake up. Brrring! goes the alarm clock. It tells us what time to get up.

In the morning, we get dressed and wash our face and hands.

We tie our shoes. Whoops, Hooligan. You pulled the laces too hard!

Breakfast is the meal we have in the morning. Pickles Pig usually eats a whole box of cereal for breakfast. He'll be sorry later.

There are chores to do in the morning. Wiggles is washing the breakfast dishes.

In the morning, children go to school. Some grown-ups go to school, too. They are the teachers.

At School

Cousin Ali is the painting teacher at school. Today he is teaching the children how to make a portrait.

Henny is the singing teacher at school. She is teaching the chicks' choral group how to sing in harmony. "I hope they learn soon," say the visitors to the class.

At Night

It is eight o'clock at night. Day is over. The sun has set, and you can see the moon in the sky. Everyone is tired from a day of working and playing. Are you sleepy? Then quick, to bed!

Big Hilda is yawning. Kitty is yawning. Only Squeaky isn't yawning. That's because he is already asleep.

Bedtime

It is night. Everyone is in bed. Squeaky has a tiny mouse-size bed. Why isn't he asleep now? Big Hilda's big yawn woke him up.

Squigley's bed isn't long enough. That's why he sleeps with his tail out the window. Chips Beaver made his own bed. That silly Chips–he forgot to make the foot part! Mose Moose has fallen asleep with the light on.

Bumbles has fallen asleep with his hat on.

Why is Pickles Pig still awake? He has a stomachache and Ma Pig is taking his temperature to see if he is sick. He probably ate too many pies for supper again.

Here's another pig in bed. It looks like he is a very restless sleeper.

Squeaky's Day

Squeaky gets up very early. It is seven o'clock. He watches the sun rise and plays on his scooter bike. Later in the morning he goes to the market to buy some cheese.

It is five minutes after twelve noon. It is lunch time. Squeaky always has cheese for lunch. That's because he is a mouse.

In the afternoon, Squeaky visits his friends and plays games with them. He has a good supper at six o'clock (cheese again). After reading a bedtime story, he is fast asleep by eight o'clock in the evening. Good night, Squeaky!

The Days of the Week

Sunday
Monday
Tuesday
Wednesday
Thursday
Friday
Saturday

Cousin Ali is telling Squeaky all about the days of the week. "You know that there are seven days in each week," says Ali. "Do you know their names?"

"Of course," says Squeaky. "Sunday, Monday, Tuesday, Wednesday, Thursday, Friday, and Saturday." Can you say the days of the week with Squeaky?

Squeaky's Week

On Sunday, Squeaky went for a drive in his car. He went to visit his grandmother.

On Monday, Squeaky had a job to do for Mrs. Fishhead. He was the only one who could do it. Can you tell why?

On Tuesday, a bee tried to sting Squeaky, but Squeaky jumped behind a glass bottle. The bee didn't notice the glass until it was too late.

On Wednesday, Squeaky went for a walk. Bully Bobcat went, too, but he didn't get far. The footbridge broke and he fell into the stream. He had to go home and change his clothes.

On Thursday, Squeaky went to a cheese cafe for dinner.

On Friday, Squeaky visited Cousin Ali Cat.
Cousin Ali drew a giant portrait for him.

On Saturday, Squeaky went to a party.
Hooligan played the fiddle, and Squeaky and
Cousin Ali danced a jig.

When the party was over, it was already
Sunday again. Time to visit Grandmother,
Squeaky.

January February March	April May June	July August September	October November December

The Months of the Year

Thirty days has September
April, June, and November.
All the rest have thirty-one,
Except February, which has
twenty-eight,
And, in leap year, twenty-nine.

Cousin Ali is telling Squeaky all about the months of the year. "You know that there are twelve months in a year," says Cousin Ali. "Can you say their names?"

"Of course," says Squeaky. "January, February, March, April, May, June, July, August, September, October, November, and December."

"Good," says Ali. "Remember 'Thirty days has September' and you'll know how many days each month has."

Yesterday, Today, and Tomorrow

Today is Babykins' birthday. He is one year old today. He is having a wonderful birthday party.

Yesterday was the day before the party. We all made presents for Babykins.

Tomorrow will be the day after the party. We will all clean up the mess.

Spring **Summer**

The Seasons

Spring begins in March and ends in June. The weather begins to get warm and plants begin to grow.

Summer begins at the end of June and ends in September. The weather is warm—it's a good time for a swim.

Autumn begins at the end of September and ends in December. It is cooler and the leaves turn beautiful colors.

Winter begins at the end of December and ends in March. It is the coldest time of the year. Sometimes there is snow!

Autumn

Winter

Spring

In spring, the earth and the air begin to warm up. The leaves come out on the trees, and flowers bloom. It's a nice time to take a walk outside and see the world waking up after its winter sleep.

Summer

The sun is shining, the sky is blue, and it is hot! Summer is the time for a vacation at the beach.

Autumn

In autumn, the leaves fall from the trees. We can rake them into a pile. Maybe our parents will help us have a bonfire. The air is cooler and the heat from the fire feels nice.

Winter

After autumn comes winter. We can go sledding or skiing if there is snow. Christmas comes in winter.

Warm and Cold Weather

When the weather is really cold, the pond freezes. A layer of ice covers the water. Squeaky likes to ice skate.

When the weather is warmer, the ice melts and the ground softens. HeeHaw Donkey plants his garden.

When the weather is hot, Squeaky and Big Hilda go swimming. The sun is shining fiercely, and swimming is the only way to stay cool.

When the weather gets cool again, it is time to get ready for winter. All the animals make sure they have enough food, and make their houses snug and warm.

HeeHaw's Weather

On sunny days, HeeHaw works
in his fields. He likes to drive his
tractor through the tall wheat.

On rainy days, he gets wet.
HeeHaw, it is silly to drive around
on your tractor in wet weather!

In stormy weather, when the thunder
crashes and the lightning flashes through
the clouds, he hides in the hayloft.

In snowy weather, he must shovel a path to the barn so he can feed his hungry animals.

In gray, foggy weather, HeeHaw can't see where he is going. Once he fell down the well. HeeHaw, you should be more careful in foggy weather!

THE
END